The
Maiden's
Sleep

Michael J. Stiehl

World Castle Publishing, LLC
Pensacola, Florida
Copyright © 2023 Michael J. Stiehl
Paperback ISBN: 9798891260825
eBook ISBN: 9798891260832
First Edition World Castle Publishing, LLC, January 16, 2024
http://www.worldcastlepublishing.com

Licensing Notes

Cover: Cover Designs by Karen
https://www.cover-designs-by-karen.com
Editor: Karen Fuller

For Scout. Gone, but not forgotten.
Forever in my heart.

Special Thank You to Adrian Simmons and Neil Baker at Heroic Fantasy Quarterly (www.heroicfantasyquarterly.com).
Thank you for teaching me the importance of naming things and calling me out for lazy fantasy tropes. Your support was invaluable.

Chapter 1

I hate kids, and yet there are two in the pile of sticks and mud I call home.

"Please help us," says the girl with hair the color of flax seeds.

Her brother stands so close to her and is so silent I wonder if he's real. I woke up with a bad case of double vision today, so it's not impossible. It took an hour of drinking to make it go away.

The only kid I ever didn't hate was my own, but I should have. My daughter killed my wife when she was born. After that, I thought I would spend my days fighting the urge to throw her in a river. It didn't work out like that.

"What's the trouble?" I say, rubbing

my eyes with grubby fingers.

"Our father is missing," the girl murmurs, staring at the dirt floor. I watch her breath turn white in the cold fall air.

"Who's your dad?" I grunt.

"Aston Ozker," she replies, expecting a reaction.

"Never heard of him," I say, denying her one.

"We haven't seen him in a week," she continues.

"Then he's dead," I reply, trying to stand, wobbling, and then thinking better of it.

"No he isn't!" the boy yells, flecks of spittle flying. The sound of his voice makes my head want to explode.

I have an urge to make sure the boy doesn't make that sound again. I consider killing him. I even grope for my bow before I remember I sold it three months back. I stare at him, backlit by the pale sunlight outside the doorway, and decide to humor him.

"What makes you so sure?" I say,

unclenching my teeth and trying to sound comforting.

"Because," he replies, pausing for a moment before continuing, "my dad is too tough." I envy the boy's certainty. I'm jealous that he still believes in something when I no longer can.

My old man was shit. I had no illusions about that from a young age. Sure, homesteading on the fringes is a hard life, and that's bound to make for a hard man, but he went further than that. There were whole seasons when I wore more bruises than clothes, and I often wondered how the hell he expected me to work all day with cracked ribs.

"What do you want me to do about it?" I ask, genuinely curious what they'll say. Why two kids would trek out here to this rundown sod house is a mystery to me. Any normal person would have run off at the sight of it, let alone the smell.

"Find him," orders the girl. "We've got money."

She fumbles in the pocket of her enormous frock coat and pulls out a small leather bag. With a lackadaisical flick, she plops it on the ground just out of my reach. It spills open, and a sea of worn copper pieces sluices across the ground. It's a paltry, laughable sum and more money than I've seen in months.

I flop over on my side, scoop up the coins and start counting. Dignity be damned.

"Monsters must have taken him," the little boy blubbers, "hidden him in Turecek Keep."

There are sixty-seven worn copper pieces and one-half of a silver piece from all the way back in Lord Elderbine's reign. It will buy me food for a month, maybe more, but I'll drink it away in a week.

"Fairy tales," I grumble, focusing again on the children. "Everyone thinks anything that goes missing around here is scooped up by monsters and taken to that pile of rocks. It's like I said, your dad is dead. Killed by bandits."

"You are Bow, right?" huffs the girl.

How do I answer that when I'm not sure anymore?

"Doesn't matter," I say, putting the coins back in the bag with my shaking hands, "not interested."

"I heard Knife and Bow help people," whines the boy. "They're heroes."

"Well, Knife is dead," I say, picturing my daughter's face, "and Bow would like to be. So piss off."

I close the bag and toss it at them, then I lay down and roll over on my side.

"Look," says the girl, desperation straining her voice, "I don't know where our dad is, but I think I know who does — Freneck."

I see my daughter, blue-faced and still. I'm crying over her body, and next to her is an empty vial. It was supposed to cure her of the Maiden's Sleep, but she hated the smell of it and wouldn't drink it. She always had better sense than me. I hid it in her food, convinced it was the right thing to do. I can still hear her rasping and trying to speak that horrible night I watched her die. "I love you," she said over and over until all she could do was point and say "you."

I'd bought that poison from Freneck.

I roll back over and sit up, almost throwing up the half bottle of booze that's sloshing in my gut. "Tell it to your mom," I say, "or Bennie or, hell, anyone but me. I'm not going to be any help."

"Our mother has been dead for years," snaps the girl, "and Bennie and the rest of the town guard laughed when we told them. We've tried everyone. You're all that's left."

The boy moves the dirt floor around with the toe of his boot before saying, "Please."

My daughter was my heart. With my wife dead, all my love moved to her and magnified. I never wanted to be without her, so I resigned my commission in the royal guard, collected years' worth of pay, and took to the road in search of a quiet life.

I was a terrible farmer and even worse at the trades. Soon, money got tight.

But then I found a way to make money with my bow again. It was an accident. I was holed up in a village overnight when thugs came looking for trouble. They found it in me. Come dawn, half were dead, and the others were running for their lives. The villagers scraped together what they had and gave it to us. Then, they told us that two towns over, they had the same problem.

I tried teaching my daughter the bow as soon as she could stand. She was terrible. Had no feel for it. But she always liked knives. At first, I thought it was because they were shiny, but that wasn't it. Killed her first rabbit at twenty paces when she was three. She only got better from there. By eight, I'd taught her everything I knew about fighting. By twelve, not a man around could best her, especially not with a knife. That's when people started calling us Knife and Bow. My daughter was always so proud of that.

I reach for the bag of coins, but the little girl grabs it first. She pours some of them onto the packed dirt floor. "Half now, half later," she says, ice in her voice.

"Okay," I mumble, scrounging the coins from the ground and knowing I'm about to be stupid. "I'll ask around, but that's all."

The kids look happy. I wish I shared their enthusiasm.

CHAPTER 2

Bennie greets me with a fist to my gut. I throw up on him and fall down.

"Fuck," Bennie grunts, "you get more disgusting every day."

Lying in the mud, only twenty paces inside Dunwynn's main gate, I hear his guards laughing. Whether it's at Bennie or me, I don't know.

"Nice to see you," I say, the taste of vomit fresh in my mouth.

"I wish I could say the same," says Bennie, holding out his hand. One of his goons rushes up and hands him a rag. Bennie starts wiping his uniform with it.

"I thought I told you to never come back," he continues, pushing globs of my puke off his sleeve.

He did. A month after my daughter died, I was in the middle of my fourth fight in a week. I hadn't killed anyone, but I'd come close. I just wanted to feel something, anything, even if it was just anger or pain. Bennie and his goons finally jumped me one night, coming out of the Laughing Loon. I hurt a bunch of them, but they had the numbers. Bennie made it clear I was bad for business and then broke both of my hands and threw me out of town.

"You know me, Bennie, sometimes I gotta be told more than once," I say with a grin.

Bennie finishes cleaning his uniform and throws the filthy rag in the street. Then he cracks his knuckles, the same way he did when we were kids, and he was Dunwynn's number one bully. I know he's going to punch me again.

"Besides," I say, trying to head it off, "I'm here on business."

"Yeah," he says, lowering his fists,

"what business?"

The only thing more reliable than Bennie punching his way out of a problem is his greed. He gets a cut of everything that goes in and out of the main gate, or else. If I've got a lead on something valuable, he's going to make me pay.

"I'm here as a guest," I say, standing. "I've been invited in by those two kids."

I turn to point at them, but they're gone. They were right behind me, had been all the way from my hovel. Now they aren't, and I look like an idiot. They probably saw Bennie coming and took off, smart enough to know him for the trouble he is.

"You're pathetic," Bennie chortles, his fat face shaking like a tray of sallow pudding. "The mighty Bow reduced to this. A piss-stained peasant."

He grabs my tunic and pulls me close with his thick fingers. I can smell what he ate for lunch and the cheap ale he washed it down with. I notice he has fewer teeth than the last time I saw him.

His free hand rummages around my tunic and then goes through my pockets, looking for anything of value. He finds the knife I keep in the back waistband of my pants and takes it. It was my daughter's and the only thing of value I haven't sold yet.

"Give it back," I say with venom.

"No," he replies, and then he pounds his fist into my face, and it feels like my head is being crushed by a ham.

He lets go, and I fall to the ground, my mouth full of spit and blood, my right eye stinging. All I hear is the muffled sound of laughing. I'm face down, hunched, like a pill bug that's been poked by a curious toddler. I can hear him breathing like a worn, old fireplace bellows. I know he's going to kick me.

"Shoulda kept your mouth shut," he grumbles. I scoop a handful of dirt and gravel from the street with the hand he can't see. I hear the grind of his boot as he wheels his foot back and spin away from him as he kicks. His massive boot misses my midsection by inches. Then I roll back, grab the heel of the boot with my free hand, and vault upward. I send him off-balance, sprawling backward. His vast bulk collides with three of the guards behind him, and they all crash to the ground.

Standing, I throw the dirt in his eyes. He screams as he rolls back and forth on the men underneath him. I take my daughter's knife back and then, for good measure, steal the club from the belt that is straining to hold back his disgusting gut. Then I'm running.

I hear him shout for his men to get me, but I already have a head start. I duck down several random alleys in a row before hiding in a discarded hand cart. I wait for a few minutes until I'm sure they haven't followed. I take a deep breath and realize I have no idea what to do next.

CHAPTER 3

Freneck is babbling. He does that.

After my run-in with Bennie, I came here. I had nowhere else to go. I looked for the kids but couldn't find them. It's probably better this way, without them underfoot. Besides, I figured sooner or later they'd find me. They know where I live.

"Tell me where Aston Ozker is," I say, blocking the only exit from the room.

It's a small room, made smaller by the piles of books, glass vials, and opaque brown jars that fill it. In the jars, I can see the shadowy outlines of various dried things, different colored powders, and other odds and ends. Exactly what you would expect from a low-rent alchemist.

"Aston?" he answers, looking surprised. "I have no idea."

I can tell I bother him. Good. I want to bash his face in, I want to kill him where he stands for what happened to my daughter, but I don't. I don't because it won't change anything. I don't because I was stupid enough to believe him.

"Funny, his kids think you do," I say, dragging my finger absently through the dust on the edge of his worktable. I watch it trace an unsteady track through the grime with the half-swollen shut right eye Bennie gave me and think about how my mangled finger resembles the crooked branch of a dead tree.

Freneck gapes like a fish on land before saying, "I'm sorry about your daughter."

I can tell he means it.

I let things get uncomfortable before I pick up a wooden spoon with a broken handle. It's jagged and full of splinters. I notice other broken things around the room: a brazier with a bent leg propped up by a small rock, a book with a half-torn cover, a window tied shut with rope.

"What's with you, Freneck?" I ask, putting the spoon down and walking toward him. "Why is your place full of all this broken old shit?" I punctuate the second question by waving a broom at him that has no bristles.

"Because it's useful," he explains.

"How? It's just junk," I say, dropping the broom on the ground to make my point. It lands with a loud clatter.

"In my experience, people undervalue broken things. Except for some books and my alchemic supplies, most of what you see in this room I acquired for nothing because someone discarded it."

"That's because it's garbage," I grunt. I pick up a bowl with a crack in it the size of my hand and look it over.

"Nonsense," he protests, snatching it from me. "That spoon is the perfect thing for propping open my window when I'm reducing liquids to powders. And this bowl?

The glaze on it is made with a mineral that is impossible to find for five hundred miles, and yet, with a little work, I can grind some from it whenever I need it."

"Well, good for you, you're the wizard of junk. Now answer my question, where's Ozker?"

"I told you, I don't know," he murmurs. "I have as little to do with him as possible."

"Why's that?" I say, getting closer to the edge of the table.

"No reason," Freneck stammers.

Behind him, a vial is perched over a small flame. Puffs of light blue smoke leap from it at odd times. I wonder what it is. In the center of the table, an oil lamp flickers, casting unsteady shadows. I put my hand close to it, feeling the warmth of its flame.

"In your line of work," I continue, "I would imagine fire is a real concern."

I bump the lamp and watch foul-smelling oil leak from it onto the tabletop.

"I'm sorry," Freneck pleads, "please

don't."

"That's twice you've apologized to me," I snap, nudging the lamp again. "Stop it."

"What do you want?" he moans, sweat on his brow, panic in his eyes.

"The truth," I snarl. I give the lamp a jolt, and this time, a wave of oil washes out of it, making a puddle. A small ember from its wick flies into the air, nearly landing in it. "Why were you avoiding Ozker?"

"Like I said," Freneck stammers, "no reason. I just don't like him, okay?"

"That feels like a lie," I reply, knocking the lamp over and watching the puddle ignite. "I really hate lies. I think you had a very good reason for avoiding Ozker, and I want to know what it is."

"Put that out!" he yelps, grabbing a pot lid and reaching for the flame.

I grab his arm as it stretches out in front of me with my mangled hand. Its impossible crookedness stands in stark contrast to the fine straightness of his forearm. I force his arm down to the tabletop, directly next to the spreading fire. It pulls his face within inches of my own.

"Quit lying, Freneck. You, of all people, know I've got nothing left to lose. Honestly, burning to death tonight might be the best thing for me. Shame if you came with."

"Okay!" Freneck exclaims. "Just put out the fire, and I'll tell you."

I take the lid from his hand, place it over the spreading fire, and release his arm. He staggers back, a mixture of relief and fear on his face.

"Ozker is trouble," he exhales, getting a hold of himself.

"Trouble how?" I say, walking away from the table.

"He's playing with things he shouldn't be," Freneck replies.

"Like what?" I ask, trying to read the spines of the books on his shelves. All of them are in languages I don't understand.

"Like interious alchemy," he says,

as though I should understand the gravity of the words. I make a face indicating my ignorance.

"Okay," he groans, skillfully pulling a book from the bottom of a teetering pile on the corner of the table. He spreads it open before explaining. "You know how the world can be described by the four arts, right?"

I indicate I don't.

"The Four Arts," he huffs before continuing, "are alchemy, mechanics, mentalism, and eschatology. Everything we see or do in the world can be explained by one of them. It has been this way since man crawled out of the cataclysm and regained his reason."

"What does this have to do with Ozker?" I say, looking at a drawing in the book. It's a picture of the world, carved into four parts and surrounded by gold leaf monsters.

"Long ago, there were Five Arts," Freneck says, looking around as though worried someone might hear. "Alchemy was divided into two schools, interious alchemy and exterious alchemy. Each is separate from the other. They became rivals and fought, with exterious alchemy winning. It was a terrible conflict, and the surviving alchemists decided that all knowledge of interious alchemy should be destroyed. But knowledge wants to live. The interious alchemic arts continued among small sects of believers, which, from time to time, were found and destroyed. They have never been rooted out completely."

"So what?" I spout, realizing I want a drink. "A bunch of alchemists want to kill each other. People will fight over the stupidest things. What's new?"

"You don't understand," Freneck says, looking up from the book, "interious alchemy is focused exclusively on the self. Its goal is to discover elixirs that change the human body, that make it smarter, stronger, impervious to pain or damage. They want to tamper with the divine. Exterious alchemy would never do such things. We are only interested in how the world works. We seek to understand and improve what lays outside ourselves."

"Is that why you killed my daughter?" I say as he closes the book and sets it down. "Because you were playing with things you don't understand?"

"No," he stammers, "to alleviate suffering falls within the virtuous alchemic arts. In the case of medicine, we are merely assisting the divine body. What Ozker and his kind do is change it fundamentally. Here, let me show you."

Freneck scuttles to the nearest wall of the tiny room. On it is a shelf with a row of leather-bound books. I notice how frail he is and wonder if he ever eats. His shaggy black hair is greasy, and his complexion is pale. His eyes seem too large for his head. I notice he's practically a kid.

He moves a few volumes aside and, from behind them, pulls a thin, hide-bound book. He brings it back to the table, and I can see burned into the front of it a title in another language I can't read. He opens it to a page filled with drawings. They seem to be of humans, but some of them have wings or extra arms, others giant skulls or huge orb-like eyes. A few seem to be exploding with muscles.

"These are sketches of a clutch of interious alchemists that were rooted out ten years ago. After they were killed, this journal was circulated as a warning. A reminder of how traveling down their path leads to horror."

"And Ozker was doing this?" I say, my eyes fixed on a drawing of a child with the torso of a spider.

"I believe so," Freneck replies, looking troubled, "and if I did, you can bet that others in the Alchimia Academia did too. If Ozker was discovered engaging in forbidden alchemy, he would be put to death. That might explain why he's missing."

That fit. It made sense that the local alchemists would want someone making monsters rooted out of their town. But something bothered me.

"If the Alchimia Academia killed Ozker, then why do his kids think you had something to do with it?"

"His kids?" Freneck says, looking baffled.

"Don't bullshit me," I say, giving the scorch mark on the table a solid tap with my finger, "my patience is thin."

Freneck looks down at the sea of black char on the tabletop, and I know I'm on to something. I let him twist for a minute.

"I didn't kill him," he says, looking up, a thin line of sweat on his brow, "at least not directly."

"Say more," I growl.

He exhales deeply before the words pour out of him. "I sold him a book on interious alchemy nine months ago," he blurts. "I came across one years back and hid it, just in case. I should have burned it, but I didn't. He was making noise all over Dunwynn about wanting one, saying that he'd pay a significant sum for it. Times were tight. I did what I had to."

"And what was the book about?"

"I told you, interious alchemy," Freneck replies, looking angry.

Something about this stinks, but I don't know what. Maybe it's just because I hate Freneck, but I can't let him off the hook. "Be specific," I press, "Why did Ozker want it?"

"He didn't say," Freneck mutters, still agitated, "and I don't know because I'd never opened it."

"Don't lie. No way a curious fellow like you doesn't peek," I say, stepping back from the table.

Freneck's face scrunches up like a kid caught stealing. He's conflicted, and I can see the wheels turning as he decides what to say next.

"Fine," he huffs, "I peeked. Okay? I looked in the book. I know I wasn't supposed to, but I did."

"And?" I say, coming around the

table to stand next to him.

"And it had something to do with human development. That's all I know. It was about controlling how bodies grow, changing that growth. I didn't look at more than a few pages."

"Thank you," I say in a soothing voice, putting my hand on his shoulder. "I appreciate your honesty."

"Sure," he says, looking bewildered by my softer tone.

"So, it's safe to say then," I continue, removing my hand and looking him straight in the eyes, "that whatever he was up to, you made it possible."

Freneck is stunned. I can see his jaw working. I can see him trying to come up with an excuse, any excuse, but in the end, his face softens, and a look of defeat washes over him. "Yes," he admits, "but I swear I don't know what he's up to or where he is. I haven't seen him since I sold him the book. I didn't even know he was missing."

"Where did you sell him the book?

Did he come here?"

"God no," Freneck says with revulsion, "I went to him. I didn't want him knowing where I lived."

"Alright," I reply, believing him, "put on your stuff."

"What?" Freneck says.

"I said, put on your stuff. You're going to take me to where you sold him that book. Right now," I answer with malice, moving toward the door.

Freneck looks terrified, and I can't tell if it's of going with me or what will happen if he doesn't. He stands, frozen, for what feels like forever. Finally, he begins gathering his things.

He's strapping on his alchemist's belt when he says, "Did you say you're working for Ozker's kids?"

"Yes," I snap, annoyed, as I open the door.

"That's strange," he continues, putting on his waistcoat and following me. "I didn't think he had any."

CHAPTER 4

Everything smells like death on this side of town. It's dusk, and the slaughterhouse is still going strong. Fall is ending, and anyone with a fat animal has pushed them into its gaping maw. There are a few terrified cows still penned up outside its towering front door, and I wonder what it's like to spend the day listening to your friends die.

Ozker's shack sits between the slaughterhouse and the river. It gets the best of both worlds that way: the stink and the run-off. A viscous pool sits in front of its door, and I tell myself it's just mud.

The place has one small window, a long step to the right of the door. Behind me, I hear Freneck breathing through his mouth.

I slide over and peek through the window's filthy pane, but I can't see anyone. I listen but don't hear anything. I guess no one's home.

Out of the corner of my eye, I see something move.

"What was that?" I say, noticing that Freneck is shifting his weight from foot to foot to avoid puddles.

"What was what?" he squeaks, and I can see he's scared.

Panic washes over me, and I decide that drying out is making me paranoid. I can't remember the last time I spent this much of the day not drinking. Then I think about how much I'd rather be face down at a pub than doing this, and my head starts to throb.

I take a step back and push on the door. It opens. I pull Bennie's club from my belt, figuring there's less chance of stabbing Freneck in the dark with it than my daughter's knife. Going in is stupid, but I do it anyway. Freneck got me curious when he said that Ozker didn't have kids. When I'm curious, I don't stop.

Enough light seeps through the milky window from the setting sun for me to see a table with a candle on it. It's in front of me, not more than a few steps, so I risk it and move further into the room. Behind me, I hear Freneck follow and the sound of him fumbling with something.

When nothing bad happens, I start rummaging around on the tabletop for matches. I don't find any. I look up at Freneck and see he's shaking a glass vial with a cork stopper that he must have pulled from his belt. It begins to glow with a clean white light.

"Handy," I grumble.

"You're welcome," he replies, grinning.

My mouth feels like there's a rag in it, and I realize I'm thirsty. Then my stomach rumbles. I've been at this for half a day, and all I have to show for it is more questions. I know I should quit right now, but instead, I creep over to the wall, where there is a small iron stove. Its crooked flue reaches up to the ceiling like a demented arm with an extra elbow. It's ice cold when I touch it.

Ozker's place is grim and filthy, but unlike Freneck's, at least it's orderly. Along one wall are the same opaque jars that Freneck had. Only these have labels I can read, and they're in alphabetical order. Chrysanthemum seeds, clay from the edge of Pavlik Pond, dried toads, quicksilver, Ozker has it all. I notice a gap in the jars around 'P' and wonder what was there. Freneck darts over and looks at the gap. "Interesting," he says.

The toe of my worn leather boot collides with something, and I look down, but I can't see what it is. "Shine your light over here," I say, waving my hand at the darkness.

Freneck does as he's told, and his pale white light reveals a man's overcoat and trousers on the floor. Near them is a woman's dress. I get closer and realize that they're expensive, and I consider making off with them, selling them, and forgetting this job. Then I notice the smashed sideboard across the room.

"What happened here?" I think out loud.

"I don't know," Freneck replies, "maybe this will help." I see him reach into a pouch on his belt, and he removes a handful of yellow powder. Without thinking, I take two steps away from him.

Freneck blows the powder out of his hand. It swirls through the air before spreading across the floor, eventually covering it from edge to edge. Then footprints begin to glow across it, and I stare at them, mesmerized. Slowly, they start to blink on and off in a rhythmic pattern, as though invisible feet are running through the room. I watch the pattern repeat a few times, taking in their story.

I know he's expecting me to say something, but I don't. Instead, I crouch low to the floor and watch as a set of small bare feet go from the table to the smashed sideboard and then as two sets of small bare feet move away from it and across the room. My eye follows them, and that's when I see the third set of clothes in a hallway leading out of the room. They're ripped to shreds, right down to a pair of leather boots.

A bright flash of light grabs my attention, and I see a set of monstrously large footprints leading away from the shredded clothes and down the hallway away from the room. As they move away, I see the two sets of small feet follow.

Behind me, I hear something fall to the ground. I turn toward the front door, expecting to see that Freneck has dropped a jar of pickled chicks or something on the ground in front of him. Instead, I see him staring at me.

"Did you hear that?" he whispers.

I stand silent, listening. I hear the cattle bellowing just before the butcher slits their throats, but nothing else. "No," I say, "come on, keep looking for anything that might tell us where Ozker is."

I turn back to the hallway and begin to move down it toward a dark room beyond. As I do, Freneck's light illuminates a small metal-bound leather chest on the ground to my left, not far from the shredded pile of clothes. It's unremarkable, the kind of thing most people would use to store tools or other common objects. A small lock has been torn off it and is lying on the ground. There is a huge handprint in the dust coating its surface. The enormous footprints blinking on and off lead up to it and then away from it and down the hall.

I open the lid and find a row of identical black books inside. I almost shut it before noticing that the spine of each book has a single golden number on it. I grab one and call Freneck over. "Shine your light on this," I say.

I begin to flip through it. It's full of dated entries. Below each are rows of carefully written symbols.

"It's an alchemic journal. We keep

them to log our experiments," Freneck says, "but I can't read the language it's written in."

"That's because it's in a cypher," I say, recognizing it from my time with the royal guard. We used codes like this to move secret messages back and forth all the time. This one was pretty standard."

"What's he experimenting on?" Freneck asks, curiosity oozing from him.

"Beats me," I say, looking up from the journal. "If I had time, I could decode it, but that doesn't mean I would understand what he was saying."

Freneck starts pushing the books in the box around. "Strange," he says, examining the sequence of numbers on the book spines, "one's missing."

That's when I hear Bennie's voice, and ice runs through my veins. He's saying my name and something about a light. He's getting closer. I see Freneck looking confused and decide I don't have time to explain. I grab his coat and pull him after

me toward the back room, hoping to find a
way out. Instead, I find Hell.

Freneck's vial illuminates another
wooden table. On it is the rotting corpse of
a young woman face down, the back of her
neck torn open where her head meets her
spine. Behind it, along the wall and fringed
in shadows, is an oversized brick fireplace.
In it are the charred corpses of other young
women, all in various stages of incineration
or rot. The wooden floorboards are soaked
with spoiled blood, and on the wall in front
of me hangs a stained cowhide smock and
an array of butcher's tools.

If Bennie finds me here, I'm through.
I panic and spin around, looking for an exit.
I see my daughter's face on a corpse in the
fireplace. I know it's not real, but it won't go
away. I want to puke. I want a drink.

The stink of the slaughterhouse wafts
over me, and I come to my senses. I notice
that Freneck is frozen, like a statue, and with
the light from his vial, I see a hole smashed
through the back wall of the room. I'm not

sure how I missed it. It's huge, the size of a giant.

Some of Freneck's powder has made it into this room because I see more monstrous glowing footprints stride toward the hole and then pass through. Behind them, two sets of small feet follow.

"Someone's in the back," Bennie growls just outside the room, "hurry up!"

I plunge through the hole and out into a gangway between Ozker's shack and his neighbor. I assume Freneck has followed because I can still see. The remains of the wall are scattered throughout the gangway, and I nearly trip over a board as I run. Behind me, I hear Bennie's great, flabby body getting winded as he chases us. When he stops, I've never been so grateful that he's a slob.

"Keep going!" he gasps between great gulping breaths. "Don't let them get away!"

I'm running in blind terror, completely unaware of my straining legs, only focused on getting out of the gangway. When I emerge from it, I cross a wide, busy street and then race into another narrow alley beyond it. The alley is lined with cracked wooden crates, garbage, and rats. I risk a look back and see that Freneck has followed. Behind him, there are half a dozen of Bennie's goons, too close for us to give them the slip.

I run a little further and realize I'm wheezing and panting. The fear is winding down, replaced by the desire to quit. My head is pounding, and my guts are lurching, and I can't remember the last time I've run this hard. I begin to think a beating by Bennie's goons might be a reasonable alternative to how I'm feeling.

That's when I hear a crash and the sound of Bennie's men crying out. I slow, risk another look back, and see that all of them are on the ground under a pile of broken crates. They are struggling under their weight like fish on a dock, furious and flapping. Then I see, not more than half a dozen strides back, two children ducking into a doorway.

"Hey!" I scream, stopping in place

and thinking that if only I'm loud enough, they'll do what I say. They don't.

"This way!" Freneck pleads, tugging my arm.

I see Bennie's men picking themselves up and know the crates have only bought us seconds. I give in to Freneck and follow his lead down a side passage. It's even narrower than the main alley, so we move single file. Ahead, I see a dead end and know we're finished. Freneck keeps going. I have no idea why he doesn't understand we're doomed.

I turn around, knowing any second Bennie's men will round the corner, and spot a huge pile of rotting food. I realize we must be behind a restaurant or an inn.

"Quick," I say to Freneck, "in here."

I jump into the warm pile and start burrowing. It's more awful than I'd imagined, but I force myself to continue. I see Freneck wonder if following me is worse than what Bennie's men will do to him. He does the math and plows into the garbage.

In seconds, we've buried ourselves

under old potato peels and half-eaten stew. We both gag a few times, almost making the other puke, before we hear Bennie's men turn down the passage, look around, and leave.

I count to twenty and then burst from the heap of putrid decay like a drowning man. Freneck is right behind me. We brush it off as best we can, but we both reek.

"Now what?" Freneck says, a moldy carrot peel perfectly balanced on his shoulder.

"We go back and find those tracks. Something big ran out of that place. I want to know where it went."

CHAPTER 5

Where it went was Zolmavaz Fields, a place I swore I'd never set foot in again.

I've always had a talent for following things. It was like I didn't even have to think about it. I could always just do it. It led me to a life as a scout in the army. After saving my commanding officer's battalion more than once, he petitioned the royal guard for my commission.

Even all these years later, having learned a lot about fighting and soldiering, it's when I'm tracking something that I'm most comfortable. This was no different. Finding that first print in the busy street had been a challenge, but from there, it had been a straight shot to Zolmavaz, Dunwynn's largest cemetery.

I'm standing in front of the towering iron gates that lead inside, and I'm frozen. It's dark now, but a nearly full moon is out, so we aren't working blind. In front of us, on the other side of the gate, rolling hills dotted with crypts, tombs, headstones, and other markers of the dead stretch to the horizon.

One of them belongs to my daughter.

We're disgusting. Filthy hardly covers it. As we made our way here, people crossed the street at the sight of us. It didn't bother me. I'm glad they stayed away, but I can tell Freneck is growing tired of our adventure.

"Why are we doing this?" he whines.

"Because this is where the tracks led," I answer.

"No, why are we even following the tracks? I think it's clear by now that whoever put you up to this was lying. I mean, you were paid by Ozker's kids, who don't exist, to find a guy, who's probably dead, who was up to something unspeakable, and now we've followed who knows what to a cemetery in the middle of the night? This is insane!"

"Maybe," I say, my eyes drifting from him to the pockmarked metal sign that hangs from the top of the gate. "Somebody killed a whole lot of girls back in that shack, and I want to know why," I continue, staring at the cemetery's name etched into the sign in a find looping hand. "If this is the only path I've got to get some answers, then I'm going to follow it."

"You have no idea what's going on, do you?" Freneck says, putting his hands on his hips.

"Do you?" I say with scorn, turning to face him.

"Part of one," he says, removing his hands and walking closer to me. "I think, based on what I saw back at the shack, someone was killing those girls for a reason. Harvesting them."

"What are you talking about?" I murmur, moving away from Freneck and forcing myself down the dirt path in front of me and through the gates.

"It's no coincidence that there was a bottle missing from the wall in Ozker's shack and that those poor girls had the backs of their heads ripped open," Freneck says, following behind me.

"Oh really," I say, only half listening. I remember carrying my daughter in a pine box on my back down this path. I wanted her funeral to be grand, but we were never the type to save.

The night before I buried her, I got black-out drunk, pressing one coin after another on the bar until darkness closed in on me. The next morning, I woke up in a panic, knowing I didn't have enough to pay the mortician or the coachman he'd hired to take her to the cemetery.

At his office, I was a mess, crying and begging. Out of disgust or pity, he let it go, instructing the coachman to take us to the entrance to Zolmavaz but no further. Once there, the coachman dumped her coffin like a bag of trash at the gate. He threw me a piece of rope and said, "Tie to front and drag," before riding off.

I couldn't bear the thought of it, dragging her like an animal carcass to the dump. So I tied the rope through a knothole in the front of the coffin and slung it on my back. I walked endlessly until I found her open grave next to a huge pile of loose dirt and a rusty shovel. I lowered her in and got to work. I said no words and prayed no prayers. There was only the sound of me grunting for hours.

"Absolutely not," Freneck yelps, pulling me from my thoughts. "The missing bottle was in the 'P' section of his materials. There is only one thing in the back of your head that starts with 'P.'"

Even without looking, I know Freneck's waiting for me to guess what starts with 'P.' It annoys me beyond words. I turn toward him and see that he's rooted in place on the dirt path, a pout plastered on his face. I glare at him with all the shame and bitterness I feel for having failed my daughter, and watch him shrivel.

"The perficiens carnem," he ventures after an awkward pause. "That's what must have been in the missing bottle. It's almost certainly what Ozker was taking from those girls."

"So what?" I say, drawing myself up close to him.

"That part of the brain is very important. It sits at the base of your skull and regulates the way your body grows and develops."

"None of that means anything to me," I say, backing off.

"It should," Freneck says, piqued by my indifference. "Perficiens carnem means perfecting flesh. There are only a couple of alchemic reasons to use it, and none of them are good. It's a tricky area of the art, with lots of room for things to go wrong. I'm worried something did, and whatever resulted from that ghoulish mistake is waiting for us in there." He points with dramatic effect at Zolmavaz.

"What are you saying?" I snarl, the words grinding out between my teeth.

"I don't think we should go in," he squeaks.

"I'm going in there, and so are you!" I roar, surprised by my anger. "The last time I walked through these gates was to bury my daughter, and that was because of your mistake. You owe me, and you know it, so stop sniveling and pay your goddamned debt!"

Freneck looks like I slapped him, like he might cry, but he starts moving. I wasn't lying when I said it. I still blame him. I can't help it. I know the Maiden Sleep was already sweeping through Dunwynn last spring when my daughter caught it. I'd seen young women sick with it, but it was just a cold until Freneck's concoction made it so much worse.

I turn my back on him and follow the tracks by moonlight. They take us down a series of weaving paths. On either side, freshly dug graves, each for a young woman, define the grip of the Maiden's Sleep even six months after my daughter's death. I notice the different markers reaching for the night sky, each signifying the status of the corpse underneath, and I wonder why they bothered. When you're dead, you're dead. Why trouble the world with your passing?

Then I crest a hill, and before me is a pool of light. It's made up of a dozen candles in tiny glass holders. The holders try to shelter the candles from the wind, but their flames are pushed and pulled anyway, causing them to flicker and sway, to roll and lurch.

There is a marker in the center of the dancing light. Something about it is familiar. I leave Freneck shuffling behind me and race to it. Once I get up close, I see there is a simple headstone, about three feet high, and on the top of it, in miniature, a sculpture of my daughter. In the colliding moon and candlelight, I see her placid face staring boldly forward, her hands regally at her sides, and a knife on either hip. Even tiny, she looks every bit the hero.

"That's right, you don't know," Freneck wheezes from behind me. "The townspeople did this after you got kicked out. Some of us come out here at night to light candles and remember her. Old Klement, the sculptor, added the statue. He said it wasn't much, but he's too modest."

I reach out and touch the headstone and feel its rough texture on my hand. I trace the statue's boot and leg with my finger, and I want so badly for it to be her. But it's not. That's when I start to cry. Heaving, wrenching sobs well up from inside me and crash out of my mouth. My legs give out, the muscles in my back cramp, and I slump down the side of the marker to the ground, snot running from my nose. I knock over a lot of candles.

I'm not sure how long I do this. Eventually, I stop.

When I pull myself together and stand up, I turn around and see Freneck is still there. He's looking at me with compassion.

"You two saved me," he says with a gentle voice. "I'm sure you don't remember. It was years ago. Knife was still a kid. It was just outside of Dunwynn. I'd been coming back from a trip to buy materials for my alchemy when I was jumped by bandits. I gave them what I had, but they beat me anyway.

"I thought they were going to kill me, but then you two showed up. Knife and Bow. In seconds, you stopped them, killed a few, and drove the rest away. I was so grateful, not just because you'd gotten rid of them, but because of how kind you were to me after. You walked me all the way back to town, even carried my things."

I stare at him and will myself to remember, but nothing comes. We did so much of that back then it all blurs together.

"I was trying to return the favor when I sold you that elixir. I wanted to save your daughter like you'd saved me. It should have worked. It had so many times before."

Freneck walks closer and puts his

hand on the tombstone in a familiar way. "I am so sorry," he continues, and I don't know if he's talking to me or my daughter.

"I cried for days when I found out," he says, not taking his eyes off the grave. "Even broke, I gave what I had to help with this marker, and I come once a week to light candles and think about her." He turns his head, his face framed by his stringy black hair, and looks me right in the eyes.

"I know what I owe you," he says.

There is such despair in his voice that I wonder how one man can contain it all. I still want to hate him, blame him, but I can see he's genuine. I can see he misses her, too. I recognize that we share the same pain.

"Freneck," I begin, not knowing what to say. "I…"

Then I hear it. A howl unlike anything I've heard before, like a strangled man screaming. It's still echoing across the graveyard when I start running toward it.

I stumble over hedges and hills, around markers and trees. A cloud passes in front of the moon, and suddenly, it's pitch dark. I trip and tumble to the ground, landing on the soft soil of a freshly closed grave. In front of me, the sound continues, so I pick myself up and keep running. It's different now. In between the gurgling screams, I hear what sounds like sobs.

The cloud in front of the moon passes, and then I see it. A monster hunched over an ugly gash in the ground next to a huge pile of dirt. In one enormous, mud-encrusted hand is the body of a young woman, her graceful back arched, her arms outstretched and limp. With his other hand, he is picking at her unraveled and flapping burial shroud as though clumsily trying to put it back in place.

She reminds me of my daughter, and for a moment, as he fumbles with the corpse and I catch a glimpse of its withered, worm-eaten face, I see her. She's smiling, a dimple on her right cheek, her hazel eyes glinting. I'm waiting for her to tell me a joke and to laugh at it before I can. Instead, the creature drops her in the grave.

The beast looks like a hulking old man with a stooped back and wrinkled, sagging skin, but it has a tiny, skewed, mismatched child's face lodged under an enormous forehead. Its huge, hairy arms and legs look like they belong on the body of a creature twice its size. Its mouth is full of jagged teeth jutting in every direction, as though adult teeth were jammed in a baby's mouth, and its skin is yellow and slick with sweat. There are great tumorous bulges all over its body, and thick gray, stunted hair sprouts like harvested wheat in patches on its distended skull.

Near its feet, I see a black book in the dirt, the moonlight making the single golden number on its spine flash. I see an alchemist belt awkwardly slung around the creature's neck. It's naked except for some rags tied around its waist.

"Aston Ozker?" I say and watch as the creature turns its hideous meat collage of a face toward me. It stares at me for a long time with its bloodshot, asymmetric eyes, and I wonder if it's sizing me up or struggling to form a sentence.

"Yeth," he gurgles, taking a step toward me. As he does, I notice several glass vials strewn across the ground behind him and a line of desecrated graves beyond.

I'm groping for words. What do I say? Nothing would make sense.

"What are you doing?" falls from my mouth.

"Being a fool," says the voice of a little girl. It's the same one that hired me. She and her brother have stepped out from behind one of the markers. She throws a bag of coins at me, and I let it collide with my chest and slide to the ground with a clank.

"The other half, as agreed," she sneers.

"Yes, good work," says the little boy creeping up behind her. "I guess you're not nearly as much of a mess as I thought."

The hulking creature that is Ozker looks at the children in horror. I can't imagine what he's afraid of, given that he's more than twice their size. Then he looks back at me, anger warping his twisted, patchwork face even more.

In a blink, he's barreling toward me. I think about running, but there is no time. I remember that I still have Bennie's club and pull it from my belt. Ozker swipes at me with his swollen hand, and I dodge out of the way, smashing it with the club. He recoils for a moment before lowering his shoulder and charging me. I pound him with the club, landing blows on his head and body, but nothing stops his bulk from colliding with me.

I sail backward through the air, gasping and gulping, the wind knocked from my body. I land on one foot and feel it twist before awkwardly cartwheeling over myself and crashing into a stone marker.

Everything hurts.

I hear Ozker roar and Freneck's yell, followed by the sounds of a struggle. I feel like Freneck is trying to tell me something, but the ringing in my ears won't let me understand what it is. I force myself to my feet, and my head swims, but I focus just in time to see Freneck thrown into the open grave.

On reflex, I throw Bennie's club at Ozker and watch as the end of it collides squarely with his tiny, twisted baby face. He wheels backward in pain, and I surge toward the grave, unsure what I'll do once I get to it.

I stand on a wooden board nearly the size of a person and peer down into the hole. The grave diggers must have put it here to keep the edges of the grave from collapsing as they filled it in. I can feel the thump of huge feet closing in behind me, and out of instinct, I duck. I hear the air above my head part as a giant fist flies through it. I drop to the ground and land on the board as a pair of massive hands seize my filthy tunic from behind.

Out of desperation, I grab the edges of the board with both hands, vainly hoping it will keep the creature from pulling me off the ground. It doesn't. Instead, it comes free, and I find myself holding on to it with both hands as I fall backward into what seems like infinite space.

There is a second of peace as I glide through the emptiness and before I land on Freneck. When I do, the board smacks me in the face, pinning me under it. Then the dirt starts to rain down, huge waves of it, and I can hear Ozker grunting as he shovels it with his massive, deformed hands.

"Under the board," I say to Freneck, dirt lodging in my mouth as I lift it to make room for him.

Freneck moans but does as I say and presses himself against me. I hold the board above my head like a soldier with a shield defending himself from a flight of arrows. I try not to think about the corpse we're trampling as bigger and bigger clods of dirt crash into it.

The board lets out a loud crack from the impact of another surge of dirt, and I'm driven to my knees. Still, I manage to hold it in place even as the grave begins to fill in on either side of us. Straining, I turn it sideways and lodge it into the soft walls on either side of us and pray it holds.

Then, there is only the sound of dirt slamming into the board and Ozker's monstrous grunting. Filth fills my mouth, nose, and ears, and I wonder if I'll choke to death before I'm crushed. Finally, everything is quiet and black. I can feel the board bend as it strains to hold back four feet of solid earth.

I'm on my knees, and I think Freneck is on his back, pressed against the corpse. I can't tell for sure because I can't see anything. The board has bought us some time, but not much. We have only moments before it collapses, crushing us and our tiny pocket of air.

Below me, I feel Freneck squirming.

"What are you doing?" I say, tasting soil with each word.

"Hold on," he grunts, annoyed.

I want to believe he has something

that will save us, but I can't imagine what it would be. This doesn't seem like a situation where magic dust or glowing liquids would help, but he's all I've got. I decide to use my misplaced hope and put my back into the collapsing board, pushing against it with all my might, willing myself to lift all the sodden earth that's on top of us. Then my knee buckles, and I hear Freneck grunt as it drives into him.

I think about giving up, but I can't. Some broken, misplaced will to live won't let me. So, I cast aside hope and funnel all my anger into pushing on the board. My anger at Ozker for burying me in this grave, my anger at the kids that aren't his kids for tricking me in the first place, and my anger at myself that I never saw one god damned bit of this coming.

The board lets out a loud snap as it dislodges from the walls of the grave.

"Now or never," I say to Freneck.

"Take a deep breath and hold it," he replies.

I'm not stupid. I do what he says.

In seconds, I feel something warm creep up my leg. It's like water, only it's seeping in every direction at once, and it's not wet. It's over my knee and then my waist, and I feel it filling in every gap between me and the walls of dirt that surround me. Suddenly, it's over my face, and I realize I can't open my mouth. Whatever it is crawls into my nose and ears. It smells like wet hay.

I can't breathe, but I feel myself being lifted through the dirt. The cracked board is stripped from my hands by the force of the movement, and when I erupt from the ground, I'm thrown through the air. I can't see or hear anything. I land on the ground and claw at my face as I realize I'm suffocating. I feel a warm, sticky goo covering my head, and I tear at it like a hungry dog who's caught a rabbit.

I rip a piece of sludge from my face and feel the cool night air against my skin. I gulp it as fast as I can, huffing in the musky hay smell of the goop. I tear the gunk from my head and neck, and I can see again. I'm covered in a sticky white liquid that's filled with dirt and bits of rock from the grave. I look around and see I'm at the tail end of a tube of hardening white foam that has erupted from the ground. Before me, Freneck is struggling to remove the substance from his face. I reach down and pull some free. He takes a deep breath and starts to laugh.

"What's so funny?" I say as I help him.

"I didn't know if that would work," he gasps.

"What was that?" I say, pulling more crusty white glop from my body.

"It should have been a simple binding solution, the kind of thing that would stick a person in place, but I supercharged it with some mink oil. It worked better than I expected."

"I'm glad something has," I say with a grunt as I sit on a nearby headstone, picking foam from my boots. "Both Ozker and the kids got away. No way to follow them now,"

I say as the clouds finally cover up the moon for good, plunging us into darkness.

"Not true," Freneck says, and I imagine him smiling in the dark. "Before he threw me in that grave, I covered Ozker with magnetic tracking dust."

I see Freneck then in the warm, emerging yellow glow of a small circular device he's holding in his hand. There is a quivering metallic arrow on its face pointing straight through me. With a satisfied look, he says, "This will lead us right to him."

CHAPTER 6

Freneck's compass leads us out of Zolmavaz and further from town. The light from it is enough for us to see each other but not the road. I'm distracted by thoughts of my daughter as I limp along on my twisted ankle. Afterwhile I decide that my nose is broken, and a bitter smirk crosses my face when I realize that my swollen eye from Bennie has a little friend.

After tripping over several roots and stepping in more than one pile of horseshit, I steal a lantern from a nearby barn. I'd rather risk the wrath of a local farmer than the indignity of stumbling and falling one more time. I realize I'm on my last nerve.

We follow the compass for a while,

and it takes us to Turecek Keep. I nearly laugh out loud that Ozker's little boy, who isn't his little boy, had been right all along. The Keep sits on a high hill looking down on the only pass through the western mountains. No one knows who built it, only that they did a damn good job and that it has saved Dunwynn more than once from a marauding foe.

Despite all that, the town regularly forgets about it, except when singing bar songs or telling children fairy tales. It's been a generation or more since anything happened at the keep. Just as long since anyone bothered to maintain it. Today, portions of it are just piles of mismatched stones, while other parts look untouched by time, ready to save the ungrateful residents of Dunwynn again at any moment.

"Why did Ozker come way out here?" I say to myself.

"Not for any good reason," Freneck replies from behind me. His response is startling; it's been so long since he's said anything, and I've been so lost in thought that I realize I'd forgotten he was there.

"What do you think Ozker was up to?" I ask, looking back at him over my shoulder but still trudging forward.

"It's hard to say," he blurts, quickening his step to catch up, "the alchemic arts can be fickle."

"Take a guess," I answer as I turn my gaze forward and dodge a tree root sprawling across the path.

"There are only a handful of things that the perficiens carnem is used for," he says, looking thoughtful, "and if I discard the ones related to sex because, frankly, Ozker didn't do himself any favors there, I'm left with metabolism and growth. Given that, I suspect he was trying to make himself bigger and stronger, maybe younger, too."

"So the usual. Some old guy trying to get back what he lost."

"It looks that way, only it doesn't seem to have worked well."

"It never does," I grumble.

Freneck and I walk along in silence until we find a pile of thorny shrubs to hide in just down the path from the main entrance of Turecek Keep. Everything about it is terrible, except the view it gives us of the main gate and that I don't have to walk on my ankle anymore.

I see a guard standing just inside the stone archway leading into the Keep. The archway is on the other side of a rotten-looking wooden drawbridge that spans a stagnant moat filled with black, glassy water. I wonder how many bodies are at the bottom of it.

After a while, he wanders out onto the bridge to take a piss, and I understand the source of the fetid smell that has been wafting our way since we got here. He looks like a demon from hell, with six-inch horns on his head, red skin, fangs, claws, and solid black eyes. The impressive fart he lets out while giving himself a solid shake is a telltale sign that he's no resident of the underworld.

I watch him buckle his alchemist belt

and see his shoulders, like a pair of massive stones, roll forward under his dark brown cotton shirt. The astonishing bulk of his arms strain against the limited circumference of his sleeves as he turns away from the moat. Both things make me reconsider going in the keep.

"Don't let it bother you," Freneck whispers. "It's common in interious alchemy to modify your body in disturbing ways. It's a sign you're serious."

"Well, we're going to have to get past Lord Serious there if we're to catch up with Ozker and those kids," I say quietly, watching the play demon shamble back into the shadows.

"I have something," Freneck says, rummaging through his belt. He pulls out a small glass atomizer and beams with pride.

"What's that?" I snort, wondering if it will shoot fire, shrink us to the size of ants, or twist us into monsters.

"It's Dagmar's Tonic of Imperceptibility," he replies with a smile, "or near enough. I couldn't afford all the materials, but I got the important ones. A little of this, and we'll be invisible."

Before I can ask him what the unimportant ingredients were for, he's spraying himself with little puffs of vapor. Puff by puff, he disappears, and it's the damnedest thing I have ever seen. After a minute, the atomizer floats over to me and is dumped in my outstretched hand. I hesitate before giving the bulb hanging from it a tentative squeeze. I don't feel anything, but I look down at my chest and see that part of me is missing. Sensing no damage, I cover the rest of my body in the mist.

We creep from the bushes, and I remind Freneck that just because the king of farts can't see us doesn't mean he can't hear us. I give him a few tips on moving quietly before we slink off. I'm halfway to the bridge when I remember we stink. I pray we're downwind.

When I get to the bridge, I can clearly see the alchemist standing, shrouded in shadow, just inside the archway. I assume Freneck's potion is still working because I watch him scratch his face for a while, oblivious. I catch a waft from the moat and know we're in the clear. No way we smell that bad.

I step onto the wooden drawbridge and notice that it's made of a light-colored wood, like oak or maple. It doesn't really matter except that it makes it very easy to see the muddy prints my boots are leaving on it.

I freeze and feel Freneck walk into me. He hits me hard enough that I stumble and take a step, leaving another footprint. Out of reflex, I hold my breath. On cue, the alchemist saunters out of the shadows toward us, staring straight ahead before pressing on the side of his nose and launching a well-aimed glob of snot onto the drawbridge.

I risk a long, slow breath through my mouth and prepare to slip past him when he says, "Did you actually think they wouldn't put the guy who can see body heat on guard duty?"

I watch as the smile crawling across his angular, red face reveals two rows of pointed white teeth. Then his massive horn-covered skull swivels the solid black orbs he sees with at something directly in front of him. "It took you long enough to come down here from that bush. I was starting to think I'd have to walk all the way over there to kill you," he says in a low rumbling voice.

Then his hands stab forward, grabbing what I can only assume is Freneck. I'm unsure where the demon alchemist has a hold of him, but judging by Freneck's strangled voice, I'm guessing it's his neck. I watch horrified as the alchemist lifts his arms upward, and I'm left to imagine Freneck's invisible body swaying back and forth, suspended off the ground.

I can see the alchemist preparing to tighten his grip, watching as his arms vibrate up and down ever so slightly due to an unseen weight wriggling and writhing before him. I can see bits and pieces of his forearms disappear and reappear as Freneck's hands grab and claw at them.

For a moment, I lose my nerve. I tell myself it's not my fight, that a bag of half-bent coins isn't worth dying over. Then I'm thinking of my daughter. Seeing her dying face in front of me again, begging for help I couldn't give. I begin to tremble with anger at my inability to save her.

"No," I say numbly and watch as the alchemist's eyes flick in my direction. There is a bright, white wave of rage welling up within me. I feel it burning in my gut, rolling outward to my limbs. I vow not to let this happen again. Not to let the light go out of another person's eyes. To have the sound of another voice disappear forever. To let someone die.

My hand reaches for my daughter's knife, but I think better of it. I worry that although we are visible to the alchemist, I still can't see Freneck and might stab him if I use it. So I grab Bennie's club instead and slam it into the alchemist's back. If it hurts him, he shows no sign of it as he calmly goes back to strangling Freneck.

Determined, I grab the club on both ends, take two steps back, run forward, and leap as high as my tired old legs will allow. I stretch out my arms and loop the club over the alchemist's head, feeling it run down the surface of his face, and I fall back toward the ground. Then I let myself hang on him like a human cape.

He drops Freneck. I can tell because I hear the thump of his body on the rickety bridge, and I see a filthy, body shaped smudge appear on its surface. He starts spinning left and right, trying to grab me. I twist away but feel my crooked, smashed up hands starting to lose their grip on the club.

I only have moments before they let go, so I plant my feet on the small of his back to keep from swinging like laundry on a windy day. It works, and I hear the demon alchemist begin to choke and gurgle. I realize I've increased the pressure on his throat, that I have leverage.

An evil grin plasters itself on my face as I tighten my grip and begin to straighten my bent legs. The alchemist flails frantically at my crippled hands, and I worry he's going to stumble off the bridge in his frantic attempt to pull the club from his throat. In a panic, I jerk my legs all the way straight in one violent movement and hear a wet snap as his windpipe is crushed.

He shakes me free then, and I tumble onto the drawbridge with an audible flop. I watch the alchemist, clutching at his own throat, turn to face me and marvel at how large his bulging black eyes have become. He's panicking now, focused only on finding some way to breathe again, so I stand up and shove him off the bridge.

I watch as he falls backwards, still holding his throat, and collides with the fetid, murky water of the moat. He goes under briefly before bursting back to the surface. He's still gulping for air, but the moat is deep enough that he has to use his hands to stay at the surface. I wonder if he'll make it to the edge of the moat or the deck of the drawbridge and find some way to pull himself out. Some way to avoid drowning before he suffocates.

But then I see a large rock, the size of my head, float off the ground by where the drawbridge meets the dirt path. It makes its way down the center of the bridge before veering toward the side where the alchemist is splashing in the water. Then it sails through the air and lands, with a solid crunch, squarely on the top of the alchemist's head. It's enough to send him below the moat's inky surface for good.

"Couldn't have him calling for help," I hear Freneck rasp.

"Not much chance of that with a crushed windpipe," I reply, feeling my racing heart slow.

"Still," is all Freneck says, and I don't need to see his face to know he has more steel in him than I'd thought.

After a moment to gather ourselves,

we move inside the keep. We wander for a bit, unsure where anything is. There are lamps and torches here and there, so someone is home. The building has a bit of a split personality, with some sections being nothing but rubble and others looking exactly as they must have when the keep was built nearly a thousand years ago. In those sections, evenly spaced, symmetrical red bricks march off in all directions, forming arched windows and curving staircases, broad hallways, and downward sloping ramps that plunge into darkness.

After a while, I ask Freneck to take out the compass, but the needle, so unerringly reliable up to this point, just spins in a slow circle. I get frustrated and wish that I wasn't invisible so he could see the pissed-off scowl on my face. We stumble around a bit more, and just as I'm about to lay into him, I hear people fighting.

"This way," I whisper, taking off toward the sound. I realize only too late that Freneck can't see me and hope that he figures out where I'm going.

I stop when I get to a part of the passageway that has a railing on the right side. A gentle light shimmers on the wall opposite it, and as I walk up to the railing, the yelling gets louder. I can almost make out what's being said. I look down over the railing and see a large circular room made of dark gray stone. In the center of it is a huge, recessed pit filled with flame, and along the walls, claw-shaped sconces hold flickering torches that cast a dancing light across the chamber.

Ozker and the kids are standing there, below me, near the great central fire pit, facing one another with daggers in their eyes. Across the pit and along the wall are a dozen robed figures. Each of them has their hoods up and their hands held in front of themselves, hidden under large cuffs. Only monastic choirs or self-important fools would dress like that, and since I don't hear singing, I figure we've found the local clutch of interious alchemists.

I think about the odds, and I don't like them. A dozen diabolical interious alchemists, or more if you count Ozker, versus a washed-up drunk and a down on his luck exterior alchemist missing half the stuff he needs to be dangerous.

I rub my mangled, crooked hands together and feel them tremble despite my best efforts. I absently scratch my face and wince as I simultaneously bump my broken nose and black eye in the process. As my ankle throbs, and something half burp, half vomit wells up in my gut, I decide that I'm not going to get mixed up in whatever's going on down there. I admit to myself that I'm not a hero anymore and decide to do the unthinkable.

"Freneck," I whisper, hoping he's nearby. "Do you have a slip of paper and some ink in your belt?"

"Of course," comes the indignant reply from right next to me.

"Give it to me," I say, holding out my hand in the general direction of his voice.

A slip of paper, a quill, and a tiny vial of ink appear out of thin air in front of me. I grab them and scrawl some instructions on the paper, wave it back and forth until the ink dries, fold it in half, and then address it. I hold the quill and vial out to him and watch as they disappear back to wherever he got them from.

The note hovers in space for a moment as he reads the name written on it.

"Are you sure?" he asks, the folded paper jangling up and down as he waves it at me.

"Yes," I reply even though I'm not, "just get back quick."

Without a word, the note disappears, and I hear his soft boots receding away from me down the brick floor of the hallway. Before he can take more than a half-dozen steps, I'm gripped by a thought. "Freneck," I whisper as loud as I dare, "how long will the invisibility last?"

"I don't know," he replies, his voice already distant, "try not to sweat."

I turn back to the yelling going on below and watch it for a while. I wish I could hear them better, but they are at least twenty feet below me and five times that far across the room. I'm only catching the odd word here and there when one of them really lays into the other.

"… Maiden's Sleep…" I think I hear one of the children say.

I lean forward on the railing and crane my head way out beyond it, unsure of what I've just heard, hoping that somehow this will make it clearer. I think I hear the little girl say, "… we only did what we had to…" just before the railing gives way.

I pitch forward into the empty air and flip head over heels before managing to grab part of the railing as it dangles in mid-air. I hang there for a minute, clutching at the smooth railing with my clumsy hands, and see both Ozker and the kids look my way. Even a few of the hooded alchemists in the back are staring now.

The wooden railing pulls free from

the mortar holding it to the wall, and I'm falling. I watch the railing careen toward the ground before it hits with a loud clack, then I land flat on my back on the dark gray stones of the chamber. I hear footsteps racing toward me as the world goes black.

CHAPTER 7

When I come to, everything hurts. I'm sitting upright against an altar with my hands tied behind my back. As my vision clears, I can see I'm close to the central fire pit. To my right, Ozker lurches back and forth from one mangled foot to another, clutching a large black book in one hand as the kids look on, smug smirks on their tiny faces.

I struggle to remain conscious, feeling my head loll back and forth on my neck, but I can see bits and pieces of my legs splayed before me. I realize that Freneck's spray has worn off in some places and that in others, the dust and filth from the fall has coated me. I wonder if the rest of me is the same patchwork quilt of visible and invisible.

I swing my head to the left and see the row of alchemists standing still like great implacable statues that have lived in this place since time immemorial. I'm much closer to all of them now, within ten feet, and as my muffled hearing clears, the sound of their voices makes my head hurt.

"Tha monsters!" Ozker bellows, pointing one of his swollen fingers at the children as he stalks about in front of the great billowing fire. He struggles to speak again, his flopping tongue colliding with the tangle of teeth crammed into his baby mouth and twists up his hideous face in the process. "Mad Maid's Sleep!" he howls.

Suddenly, I'm wide awake.

"Of course we did," barks the little girl, "because we knew you wouldn't!"

"You always lacked grit, Ozker," chimes the boy in a snotty tone.

A ringing begins in my head, and it's not from the fall. I can't focus on anything around me, and my emotions are a jumble as I take stock of what I've heard.

Was the Maiden's Sleep created by these two children? Are they really the reason hundreds of young women are dead?

"Freneck didn't know," I mumble, pieces of the puzzle slotting together in my mind.

He had no idea what he was dealing with. No idea it was something unnatural. Maybe he could have saved my daughter if he had known, maybe not. Either way, none of it was his fault.

Then, every evil thought I've ever had about him flashes through my head, and each one becomes a giant brick of guilt. I stack them on myself, one on top of another until I'm crushed. I am so sorry, and I want to tell him that to his face, but I can't because he's not here.

One of the looming alchemists begins moving forward, and I'm pulled away from my thoughts. He is a towering figure and the only one draped in a flowing crimson robe. There is a black chord cinched around his waist, and on each wrist, an ornate gold bracelet. Within the black void of his hood, two snakelike eyes loom, reflecting in the torchlight.

"Oh, Ozker," he says in a soft, deep parental tone once he's moved around the fire pit. He reaches out and gently touches the alchemist's deformed face, whispering, "What have you done?"

"Am surry Mast'r Toman," says Ozker, lying the large book on the floor and prostrating his hulking, misshapen form. "Tak," he slurs, "has fumula, noths."

"Does it?" Toman replies with a mocking tone. He picks up the book and begins walking around his penitent apprentice, taking him in with his hypnotic eyes. Then, without stopping, he opens the book and begins skimming its pages.

"You have made quite a mess," he says, still circling, "a mess you've brought to my house."

Ozker's hideous eyes flick up toward Toman, and I see fear in them before they return to staring at the floor.

"First, you bring these arrogant children," Toman says, standing still in front of Ozker, "and now," he flicks his wrist dismissively at me, "this."

"We are not children," barks the little boy.

"No, you're both vile pieces of shit," I grumble.

The little boy glares at me, and I can tell he wants me to shut up, so I decide to keep talking.

"You murdered my daughter," I say, fixing my eyes on him, "and you better kill me, or I swear I'll slit both your throats."

I summon a huge wad of phlegm and spit it at the boy. It hurtles through the air and splatters across his tunic. I smile as it slides down the front of it.

The boy covers the space between us in three quick steps and smacks me in the face hard. I crash to the ground, and as I do, I feel a sharp pain as my wrists grind across the hilt of my daughter's knife. I don't know how Toman and his alchemists missed it, and I wonder if it's remained invisible despite my fall. As my wrists throb, I have an idea.

"We are Halsan and Malanya Kovac," the boy says with pride as he straightens up to look taller.

"Is that supposed to mean something?" I say, genuinely lacking any knowledge of who he's talking about. Dunwynn may be a provincial town, but it's not without its nobility. Lords and ladies who prance about in fine clothes, attending each other's parties. For the first time, I find myself wishing, just this once, that I'd given the slightest shit about all that.

"You really are a worthless old drunk," he says, glaring down at me before giving me a solid kick in the ribs. Then he turns his back and saunters off.

I let out a gurgling gasp and roll onto my back. As I do, I make sure to block my hands from their view with my body.

"Makes sense," I wheeze through gritted teeth as I crane my neck upward to stare at them. "You two are just rich enough to think behaving like brats is normal." I smirk, spitting some blood on the floor before continuing, "You're probably also just selfish enough not to have any kids and just old enough to spend your nights worrying about what will happen to your gold when you die."

"Not anymore," Lady Kovac chirps in a superior voice. She plants her hands on her hips and sticks out her chin as if inviting me to admire her youth.

Toman starts laughing. It's a thin, rasping sound that puts ice in my veins. He's staring directly at the Kovacs as he does it, his reflective eyes squinting slightly as they float within the blackness of his hood.

"It is said that the art of alchemy reveals things as they are, not as we would like them to be," he hisses, pointing a half-crooked finger at the Kovacs. "Never has that been truer than with you two."

I use the rope to slide the knife out of its sheath and, in the process, carve up my back with its hilt. I wince once in the process and hope no one notices. I feel it come free and carefully start moving the rope across its razor-sharp blade. I can feel it working, but I need more time to cut through it completely. I can see the Kovacs are offended by Toman, but they swallow their pride. They need him.

"We'll share what we've learned," Lord Kovac says, trying to make his squeaky voice sound manly. "If you make us adults again."

Toman turns his back on the Kovacs and lowers his gaze to Ozker's miserable form. If the Kovacs expected him to show interest in their offer, they must be disappointed. Without any indication that he heard Lord Kovac, Toman kneels in front of Ozker. Gently and with grace, he touches Ozker's swollen forehead. "Rise," he says with a gentle voice.

As he stands, Ozker's hideous bulk seems to endlessly unfold. Toman only comes to the bottom of his oblong head, but even so, he is clearly in charge. "Do you know what your flaw is, Aston?" Toman asks, staring directly into his disciple's mismatched eyes.

"No," Ozker whispers, his gaze avoiding the face of his master.

"You lack vision," Toman continues. "In all the years I taught you, I could never get you to see past the obvious. You were never able to stand on my shoulders and take alchemy anywhere new."

"Am sorry," Ozker sobs, "will d'better."

"Lord and Lady Kovac," Toman says, sweeping his arm toward the two children and raising his voice, "created the Maiden's Sleep in a tenth the time you were my apprentice. They were driven, creative, and ruthless. All things a good alchemist should be."

I can feel another part of the rope give way. I'm shredding my back with the hilt now as I continue grinding the rope against the metal blade, but I don't care. Something about Toman's body language tells me I'm running out of time.

Toman reaches out his left hand and places it on Ozker's shoulder. His fingers are long and clean. There is a gold ring on one of them with a bright blue stone in it. I watch it flash in the dancing light of the fire. "These thoughtless amateurs, trained only by your meager alchemic skills, quickly moved beyond you once they realized your limits," he says with his resonant voice. "They craved a solution to their problems and cobbled one together from the second-hand books that clutter your disgusting shack. In the process, they achieved something significant, although they are too dim to recognize it. But you see it, don't you?"

Ozker is sputtering and weeping now. It's not a good look.

"It, it m'fault," he stutters, "that g'rls die. I nev'r think of it, 'til later."

"Yes, yes," says Toman, "you were so happy to have what you needed to prove yourself you never asked where it came from."

Ozker lets out a huge sigh before saying, "Only knew f'sure at Zolm'vaz. Ran test, then knew th' did it. Stop 'hem," he pleads, tilting his mismatched head down toward Toman. "Not let happ'n 'gain."

In a flash, Toman's right hand lashes out at Ozker. When he finishes, I can see the sharpened claws sprouting from the end of his fingers glint as they slowly retract. Blood pours from Ozker's neck, and he pitches sideways to the cobblestone ground.

"Pathetic," Toman says, casually opening the book and leafing through it as he moves across the room toward the Kovacs. For the first time, I see fear on their tiny faces, and I'm glad.

"So, you would like an exchange," says Toman to the Kovacs without looking up.

"Yes," Lord Kovac pipes, "we have the formula for eternal life and the material to make it." He holds up an opaque jar, and I recognize it from the wall in Ozker's shack.

I can't read the label from where I am, but I make out enough to guess it says 'perficiens carnem.' When no one reacts, Lord Kovac pauses and self-consciously looks at his tiny boy's hands before continuing. "Restore us, and we will give you a gift beyond value."

Toman closes the book with a loud snap. The room is silent for a moment before he says, "Do not presume to know what I value."

He walks toward the Kovacs and stops less than an arm's length from them. He pulls back his hood to reveal a handsomely structured face haloed by a brown mop of hair. His snake eyes are a perfect match for his scaly skin, and I can't help but wonder if there is a forked tongue perched behind his perfect teeth.

"I already know how to cheat death," he says, pointing a finger at the children, "and in a far more elegant way than you. What you offer is worthless."

I keep grinding the rope against the blade, but it's not giving. I pull at it, hoping it's weak, but it holds. I consciously control my breathing, telling myself not to panic, reminding myself of all the tight squeezes I've gotten out of over the years. Then I remember I wouldn't have survived any of them without my daughter, and half laugh that it's her knife helping me now.

"Don't let him sell you short," I yell, honestly having no idea what I'm going to say next.

"Shut up," Toman says without looking at me.

"You do have something he wants," I say, "otherwise, he would have killed you already."

The Kovacs look at me as though seeing me for the first time. Their little kid faces almost look innocent, and suddenly, I don't feel so bad for being duped by them.

"Shut up," Toman says again, turning toward me and raising his right hand. I watch as claws slowly grow from his fingertips.

"Killing me would be a mistake," I say, mustering as much bravado as I can.

"How so?" Toman replies, lowering his arm slightly.

I need more time. I'm close with the ropes. Just a few more bits are left before they break. "Because, unlike them, I know what you want, and I can give it to you," I say with a lopsided smile.

"And what do I want?" Toman says, his arm falling to his side as he takes a single step in my direction. I can tell by the look on his scaly face that I have one shot at this. One shot at keeping him interested long enough that I can escape before he kills me, but my head, absent the comforting numbness of liquor, is throbbing and not a fertile place for creativity at the moment.

"Ozker was an old man with something to prove," I say, hoping that if I lay everything out, I can buy myself some time, "and his ego got the best of him. He left you and your cozy little clutch to make a name for himself. To prove your opinion of him wrong."

Carefully, I pull at the rope binding

my wrists and feel a strand of it snap. I hope to God that Toman can't see what I'm doing.

"Desperate, he found two suckers with deep pockets who wanted to cheat death." I flick my eyes at the Kovacs, and they glare back. "So, knowing that you found a way not to die, Ozker figures it can't be that hard, only he's not that good at alchemy, and his patrons want something more than just not dying. They want their youth back."

"This is tiresome," says Toman, taking another step toward me.

"So Ozker starts recklessly asking around town for books on interious alchemy," I say, ignoring Toman, "and with the Kovac's money, he ends up building a decent library of them in his shack. Unfortunately, one after another, they all lead to the same problem, the perficiens carnem." I feel the rope give some more and know I must keep Toman staring at my face. I can feel my wrists ache from the strain, and blood oozes from my back as it seeps from my lacerated flesh.

"That idiot Ozker wanted to give up," Lady Kovac snarls. "One little obstacle and he folds. He would go on and on that it was one thing to retard the passage of time but quite another to turn it back."

"Worse yet," Lord Kovac chimes in, "not just any perficiens carnem would do."

"You needed a woman's," Toman grumbles, turning away from me and toward the Kovacs.

"Yes," says Lord Kovac, the corner of his mouth bending upward in a cruel smile, "a young woman's at that. Ozker said it would be impossible to find enough dead girls to get what we wanted."

"So, you made the Maiden's Sleep," Toman says, and as it drops out of his mouth, I understand the cruel, utilitarian horror of it. I can see the simple logic that leads from problem to solution, never mind the cost.

"We explained it all to Ozker," says Lady Kovac, "after the first girls started dying. He asked so many questions. I remember him scribbling in one of those journals of his, asking us more and more about it. At first, I thought he was proud of us, but once we finished, he looked pale and sickly."

"And yet, he went ahead with it anyway," I spout, damning myself for a lack of impulse control. Toman is still close enough that I can smell the lavender incense that coats his flowing red robe. I pray he keeps his attention on the Kovacs as I continue dragging the rope across the metal blade.

"You act like he had a choice," burbles Lord Kovac. "Forget the money. By this time, we would have happily turned him over to the town guard if he didn't do what we wanted. He could have howled all day about how we were complicit, but our money and reputation would have seen to it that no one would have believed him."

"But he made a mistake," Toman says, his back still turned to me as he takes a small step toward the Kovacs, and I picture those piles of clothes on the floor of his shack.

Then the rope breaks and my hands are free. My heart races as I think about moving, jumping up, and making a break for it, but I realize that Toman is still close enough that his razor-sharp claws would cut me down before I could get away. I force myself to be patient.

"Yes," Lady Kovac says in a clear voice. "We all agreed to drink the potion together. We figured it was the only way we could know he wasn't going to poison us. It felt amazing at first, that rush of youth, but then it went too far. It didn't take long before all of us were standing around, children in adult clothes."

"We told him to calm down," Lord Kovac says, "to get himself together, but he just couldn't keep a level head. Kept babbling that he could fix it. He mixed up another dose on the spot and said he'd try it on himself first to make sure it worked. We tried to stop him, begged him to think it through, but he gulped it down anyway."

"We knew something was wrong right away," Lord Kovac continues. "He started howling in pain and thrashing about. He became misshapen. One swipe of his massive arm sent me flying across the room into a cabinet. He nearly knocked me out."

"It was terrifying," Lady Kovac continues. "By the time I pulled my husband out of what was left of that cabinet, Ozker had stumbled over to the chest where he'd been keeping his notes. We watched, terrified, as he grew to an enormous size and let out a pitiful howl. Stumbling in his new, larger form, he flipped open the chest and fished out that journal. He was very confused and staggered into the backroom of the shack, eventually crashing through the wall. We tried to run after him, but our legs were too short to keep up. By the time we followed him out into the passageway behind the shack, he was gone."

"And that's why you hired me," I say, watching Toman turn his attention back in my direction.

"Yes," says Lady Kovac, "we needed someone to find Ozker. He was the only one who knew how the formula worked. But we couldn't use anyone we knew because they wouldn't believe it was us."

"Or they'd ask questions we didn't want to answer," Lord Kovac grumbles.

"I don't care about Ozker's failed formula," Toman says, his scaly face indecipherable as his serpentine eyes bore into me. "You said you knew what I wanted and could give it to me. So far, I've heard nothing that makes me think you do."

"What you want is in that journal, only you can't read it," I say, staring past Toman to look for a way out. I hold my wrists tight together and slightly out of sight, hoping he doesn't notice the lack of rope around them as I sit more upright.

"Ozker wrote down everything he knew about the Maiden's Sleep in a cypher," I continue, fixing my gaze on Toman's smug face. "The formula you want is literally in your hands, only you're too stupid to know how to use it. Must be frustrating."

"Careful," Toman's deep, silky voice warns as he lazily points a finger at the bleeding lump that used to be Ozker.

I see Lady Kovac think for a moment before it dawns on her. "You want to be the hand of death," she says breathlessly.

"Death with precision," Toman answers, "that's real power. With a modified version of the Maiden's Sleep, we could wipe out all the firstborn sons of a village or all the able-bodied men. Kingdoms would tremble as we killed whatever they held most dear with a wave of our invisible hand."

"We could give that to you," Lady Kovac exclaims. "It's not just in the journal. It's in our heads."

"Let me ask you a question," I say, an idea clawing its way through the fog in my brain. I beckon Toman closer with a nod of my head. He takes a long step in my direction until he is so close I can see the individual threads that make up the black cord he uses as a belt.

"Who would you rather do business with," I say, mustering a lopsided smile, "two backstabbing, entitled jerks who are sure they're better than you or a dirty old drunk looking for some booze money?"

Toman is still turning my question over in his head when I burst to my feet and grab the journal. Before he can react, I drive my shoulder into him and put him on the ground. Then it's chaos. I still don't see a way out of the room, but I run for the far side anyway, scanning the dark shadows covering the walls, hoping one will appear.

Behind me, I hear Toman yell, "Stop him!" and then I hear the pounding of boots, the clatter of hooves, and, I think, the beating of wings.

I plunge forward, still unable to see an exit, terrified by my pursuers. I imagine all the ways they would torture and twist my body for fun if they caught me and my feet move faster. Then, torchlight reveals a doorway I hadn't seen before, and I shoot through it. I look back and, framed by the archway, see the alchemists silhouetted by the great flickering fire of the central pit. They appear as a jumble of writhing and flapping, one hideous pulsing mass.

I turn back in time to see the base of a set of stairs. I vault up them two at a time, nearly dropping the book in the process. Silently, I curse my crippled hands and their weak grip.

When I reach the top of the steps, I turn right and spring down a wide red brick hallway. It looks familiar, and I turn on the speed, making my way to where I remember a passageway that led out of the Keep. I see it at the end of the hall—another arched doorway with stairs going down—and my hopes rise. Then I see the Kovacs step through it, each holding a wicked-looking dagger, and I wonder how their tiny child legs beat me here.

I skid to a halt just in time. Lord Kovac swings at me with a pint-sized boy arm, his blade whistling as it slices through the air. Another inch, and I'd have been gutted. I realize they've made the calculation that without me and the journal, Toman has to deal with them.

I look to the right and block a blow from Lady Kovac with the journal. The tip of her dagger gets stuck in the cover, and I give it a hard twist. The blade is ripped from her hand, and I can't help but feel guilty as her little voice lets out a loud cry when I give her a hard kick in the stomach.

I know Lord Kovac is coming up behind me, so I crouch down and watch as his dagger swings over my head. I pull Lady Kovac's dagger from the book and spin around. Lord Kovac is off balance, so I punch him in the face with the butt of my blade and watch as his button nose explodes in blood. He yelps and flails backward but recovers fast enough to block my exit with a wild swing.

I jump back and find myself up against the bottom of an open archway. It looks down onto the bridge and moat two stories below. Lord Kovac has closed on me, and there is a loud clank as I block his slashing swing with my blade. He's off balance again, and this time, instead of striking him, I grab his too-large coat and pull him toward me, jamming him headfirst into the base of the wall. He bounces off and slides to the floor, unmoving.

Then Lady Kovac slams into me from the side. The weight of her body nearly drives me headfirst out of the open archway. I try to throw her off, but her grip is strong, and she won't let go. She's clawing at me, relentlessly trying to get the book, and as I struggle to keep it from her, I turn to the right and see the alchemists charging down the hall, Toman and his bright crimson robe in the lead.

That's when I hear the thunder of boots marching. I look out the archway and see Bennie and a squad of the town guard barreling up the dirt path to the keep. In moments, they'll be at the bridge and then inside the Keep.

"Give me that book!" Lady Kovac

yells, clinging to me like the bloodsucking parasite she is. That's when I realize that Bennie won't save me before either Lady Kovac gets lucky, or the alchemists do, and a desperate idea forms in my mind.

"Shut up," I yell, grabbing her by the hair. I try to wrench her free, knowing what I'm about to do is insane, but she won't let go. I give up, and seconds before one of the alchemist's clawed hands can reach me, I leap out of the archway and into the air.

I hear Lady Kovac scream as she comes with me. The fall takes longer than I thought, and as we plummet, I try to will us into the moat. Her extra weight causes us to tumble, and I can just make out that we are headed for the bridge. I twist as hard as I can and place Lady Kovac behind me. We slam into the edge of the bridge, and I hear her scream cut short by a snap and gurgle. It feels like someone has kicked me in the back, and I ricochet off the bridge and into the revolting black murk of the moat just as Bennie and his goons cross it.

I black out, and when I come to, a meaty hand is fishing me from the water. It's Bennie's, and he has a stupid smile on his face.

"Somehow, you look even shittier than the last time I saw you," he smirks.

"Yeah, not all of us can be as handsome as you," I reply, watching his face puzzle out if I've insulted him.

Behind me, I can hear the racket of a huge fight. Men are shouting and, beasts are shrieking, swords are clanking, and wings are flapping. Sitting on the edge of the moat, I turn to look at the keep, and I can see a steady stream of Bennie's men entering it. The alchemists are putting up one hell of a fight, but Bennie has the numbers. It will be over soon.

"You looked real heroic falling out that window," Bennie says. "Who'd you land on?"

I look over at the bridge and see the body of Lady Kovac still hanging from it, her back clearly broken and her eyes wide open.

In the moat, I can see the journal floating.

"Nobody," I say.

Bennie shuffles his feet, and I can tell he's getting ready to say something. I beat him to it.

"No need to thank me," I say, reaching into the stinking moat and grabbing the soggy journal. "I was just doing my duty, letting the town guard know about the keep. I imagine it will make you look pretty good, though."

"Yeah," he says, dropping the pretense of being somebody important for a moment. "I appreciate it. And as a sign of my gratitude, I'm giving you another day to get the hell out of town."

"Thanks," I say, standing up, "that's generous."

The air of self-importance washes back over him, and without a word, he turns his back on me and walks off over the bridge into the keep. The fighting is nearly over, and I suspect he wants to get in on the easy action so people remember he was there.

I see Freneck down the dirt road rubbing his hands together, looking nervous. My back feels like I've been run over with a cart, and my ankle still hurts like hell. I do my best to look tough, but I end up limping to him, hunched over like an old man.

"You okay?" he asks when I get close.

"No," I reply. "You?"

"Not so bad. It was a brilliant move dragging Bennie into this. I'm sure he's going to steal anything of value out of that place before he reports it to his superiors."

"I was counting on that when I wrote the note. I knew he'd find greed more compelling than virtue." I open the water-logged journal. All the ink used to document the creation of the Maiden's Sleep is running down the pages in great blue droplets. It's as though the book is crying.

CHAPTER 8

I watch the inside of my shelter burn, its wet mud and sod exterior holding in the flames. I've taken everything of value from it, which isn't much, and I enjoy watching it go.

Freneck is standing next to me, holding the reins of a small and capable mule. It sags under his books and alchemic materials. This is his version of packing light.

"Seems a bit extreme," he says, indicating the fire.

"I only wish I could burn the sod, too," I say without looking at him.

He's right, there's no sense in burning the place, but it feels good to do it anyway. I want to erase the time I spent curled up in that hole, the time I spent wallowing in pain and guilt. There are no good memories there.

"How are you feeling?" he asks, and I find myself grateful anyone cares.

"Better," I say, actually meaning it. It's been a few days since the interious alchemists were captured or killed at the keep, and I've managed to not drink any booze. I'm not making any promises, but this is starting to feel like a pattern.

"They gave Bennie a medal," Freneck says, grabbing my small bag of possessions from the ground and attaching it to the already overburdened mule.

"I'm sure he loved that," I say, imagining Bennie's flabby face with a big, self-satisfied smile on it.

"He did," Freneck says. "It helped take some of the sting out of the mayor allowing you back into Dunwynn."

"You know," I continue, looking squarely at Freneck, "you don't have to share your new place with me. I'll figure something out."

"How could I not?" says Freneck with a smile. "After all, without you, the Alchimia Academia would never have given me an apartment to work from, let alone a stipend to live on. Turns out they were very grateful for the way we cleaned up a potentially embarrassing mess for them."

I look at the brand-new bow tied, unstrung, to the side of the mule.

"You shouldn't have bought that," I say. "I can't use it with my hands the way they are."

"You never know," Freneck says with a slight smile, "anything is possible."

I look at the bow as we slowly walk down the dirt road to town, and I wonder if I will ever learn to use it again. I think about different ways to pull back its string with my gnarled hand and about whether my arm will ever stop trembling enough for me to aim it.

Then, the thought enters my head that, for the first time in a long time, I'm entertaining the idea of living. The idea that hope is possible and that there is a future worth being a part of. I know my daughter is gone, but her spirit is still within me, pushing me to be more, to be better. For her, I will try.

The End

Michael J. Stiehl writes speculative fiction of all varieties, from fantasy to horror to weird westerns. Frankly, there is just no telling what he'll put on the page next.

Michael is a full-time staff member and adjunct faculty at the University of Chicago. With a lifelong passion for fiction, in particular horror, comics, adventure, and science fiction, he is thrilled to be pivoting away from academic publications and towards the kind of fiction that has always inspired him.

Michael lives in the Chicago suburbs with his

wife, two kids, and their very silly poodle Jack. When not writing fiction, Michael spends his time riding bikes, camping, reading books, obsessively listening to music, and playing D&D with his friends. In short, he hasn't changed at all since junior high.

Michael's work has previously appeared in the Rogue Blades Entertainment anthologies, "Reach for the Sky," and "No Ordinary Mortals." He has also been featured on the Night Shift Radio Story Tellers series, and his novella "Sanctuary" was recently published by Black Hare Press.